TACENDA LITERARY MAGAZINE

SPRING 2013 EDITION

EDITOR-IN-CHIEF
Claire Callahan

CONSULTING EDITOR
Robert Johnson

COVER DESIGN
Liz Calka
Carla Mavaddat

TEXT DESIGN
Sonia Tabriz

BleakHouse Publishing
2013

BleakHouse Publishing
NEC Box 67
New England College
Henniker, New Hampshire 03242
www.BleakHousePublishing.com

ISBN: 978-0-9837769-5-6

Printed in the United States of America

A Note From the Editors

TACENDA: n., pronounced ta'KEN'da
'things better left unsaid'

They say you should write what you know. By writing honest portrayals of the world as you see it, you will offer others the means to relate to each other and connect though shared human experiences. For the past eleven years, *Tacenda Literary Magazine* has championed this effort. With each issue, *Tacenda* has increased the public's understanding of some of the most isolated and misunderstood corners of American society. The short stories, poetry, and diaries featured in the Spring 2013 special topics issue of *Tacenda* further that effort by bringing us down the darkest corridor of the American prison system – death row.

The writings you are about to explore provide an intimate look at the expansive, tangled web of players who either operate or are caught in the cogs of the state-sponsored machinery of death. Together, these creative works investigate the harsh realities of crime and capital punishment, realities many would well prefer "left unsaid," including: racial injustice, violence, wrongful convictions, mental illness, abuse, coping mechanisms, last meals – and perhaps the most sobering of all to a literary audience – last words.

The majority of the pieces in this issue were compiled from the work of nine American University honors students studying the death penalty in an American University honors colloquium taught by Professor Robert Johnson. These students translated the academic and literary insight they gained into the world of capital punishment to produce original, thought provoking narratives and poetry. The emotional depth and distinct voices of the authors featured in this issue reveal the larger moral dilemmas we grapple with when the state kills in the name of justice.

Poems like "Prison Chef" by Elizabeth Rademacher and "If the Jury Was the Executioner" by Jada Wittow illustrate some of those dilemmas from the perspectives of the prison chef who prepares the inmate's last meal and the executioner who administers his death. These poems transport us from our roles as passive bystanders into active participants in the death house, giving us a clearer view of what it means to directly participate in an execution. "The Cost" by Philip Cardarella and "Troy" by Monica Sok then invite us to investigate the effects of capital punishment on our society. Cardarella and Sok's poetic analysis of the human errors and racial biases that pervade the criminal justice system question whether capital punishment can ever be just.

At the heart of this issue are the themes of grief and loss as they are experienced by the community, the victims' family, and the criminal offender. In "Purple," Zoé Orfanos delicately peels back, one layer at a time, these complex emotions from the perspective of each person left behind to live with the deep wound that is left in the wake of the loss of a loved one. The other short stories in the issue, "Published" by Lyndsey Grubbs and "Tripping" by Adam Bradley, and the diary entries, "Reflections of a Murderer," by Alexandra Olson, continue that examination, providing us an intimate look into the minds of those who commit incomprehensible crimes. Their powerful portrayals of the men and women condemned to die in prison (either by lethal injection or a life sentence) help us to recognize the pain and loss they experience as human beings deemed too monstrous to continue to live among us.

In the most personal work featured in this issue, "Death Row Days," Qahhar Ali Cush takes us through a day in his life in solitary confinement, awaiting a possible death sentence. Cush's raw, hour-by-hour account of his daily life in solitary details the profound human suffering experienced in the most oppressive prison settings, where prisoners struggle with violence, mental illness, and hopelessness. Finally, Marc Estes and Robert Johnson's stage adaptation of the short story, "The Practice of Killing,"[1] takes us into the death house for an unusual look at the final countdown to death that marks the culmination of the execution process.

The collection of these insightful works invites us to reflect upon our involvement, direct or indirect, in the killing of fellow men and women, and to examine whether this violence can ever be fair or just. These works show us the reality of life and death in the death

---

[1] "The Practice of Killing" by Robert Johnson won first place for fiction in a national writing contest sponsored by Wild Violent Magazine. The story is reprinted in the book, Lethal Rejection: Stories on Crime and Punishment (Carolina Academic Press, 2009).

house from many vantage points, from the chef who prepares an inmate's last meal, to the executioner who must administer the fatal injection on our behalf, to the victims' families, struggling to find peace after senseless acts of violence, and finally, to the condemned who struggle to live under the weight of their impending death.

Claire Callahan
Editor-In-Chief

Robert Johnson
Consulting Editor

TABLE OF CONTENTS

Music

Monica Sok

I visit the animal in his cage,
a cold shelter of bars and chains.
The closer I go,
ice forms at my fingertips
and I peer through the mesh screen
to discover eyes like mine
bound to a tight vigil
of this waiting place.
In the corner, he sits
tracing the lines on his hands.
He asks me for music
so I sing for him psalms,
as the ice and bars melt between us.

DEATH ROW DAYS

Qahhar Ali Cush

You asked me to describe a day in the life on death row. As I shared with you on Tuesday, it is sort of difficult to describe and then present it to anyone as torture or hardship. I will do my best to properly convey what a day on death row is like and maintain the spirit of the experience.

At approximately 5:50AM the doors on the wing slam shut and I know that the Restricted Housing Unit guards on the 10-6 shift are leaving and the 6-2 shift will be coming on duty. I'm in a single person cell. The cell is literally all concrete and steel. The bed I was sleeping on is a concrete slab with a thin mattress on it. The walls are cinderblocks three-quarters of the way around, but the front of the cell is a wall of steel bars from left to right. Imagine the old style western cells with the whole front open to look right into the cell with no privacy and that is exactly what this cell looks like today. The toilet is right next to the bed and built into the back wall. The toilet and sink are a single unit of brushed steel. I must wash and drink water from the same sink-bowl above the toilet. There is a metal cabinet affixed to the wall at the front of the cell for personal property to be put into, and there is a cement table right beside it for me to put my food tray on. A plastic chair completes the furnishings of the cell.

When the shift changes at 6AM, a guard comes around to take a list of those who want to go out to the dog kennel-run like exercise yards that I can go to five days a week for two hours a day. The two days a week that I do not get an opportunity to go to the yard I am confined to the cell for twenty-four hours. There is no shelter from the weather elements when there is inclement weather so on rainy or snow days I am confined to the cell for many days straight without even a brief relief.

Going to the exercise yard is a risk at times because then a person can be subjected to attacks from guards or prisoners. Many people are damaged mentally from their long term stays in the RHU.*
This applies to guards and prisoners. Recently there has been a number of savage attacks of prisoners throwing feces and urine on

each other. I was in a cage that was right next to two men throwing feces and urine on each other with wild abandon. Over the years I've been attacked by guards and prisoners at different times when going to the yard, but I refuse to give up the little opportunity to go out of the cell. So I've always kept in mind that I would not allow others to instill any fear into me that would cause me to sit in the cell for years without going to see sunshine and get fresh air. Many, many others refuse to go out because they fear being attacked or even being innocent bystanders who are hit with feces and urine, or attacked in some other way. There are men who have not been out in the exercise yard for ten or more years. We do not have an indoor recreation area.

Breakfast is brought to the cell by the guard because we are not allowed out of the cells for anything. I usually do not eat breakfast or lunch. I eat one meal a day and that is usually the evening meal. The food menu has been the same for many years without improvement or a break in the monotony. The food quality is so bad that the majority of men here have high blood pressure and/or diabetes. The restricted movement and poor food is in itself a death sentence.

I prefer to take each day as it comes. I do not have a program or pattern to what I do. Some days I get up and read; other days I paint while there is a degree of sunshine coming from the hallway. There are no windows in the cell and the only natural light comes from windows across the hall from my cell. The light in the cell is a florescent light and it has destroyed my eyesight over the years. I spend most of my time reading and that has caused me to burnout my retinas, and put enormous strain on my eyes. Reading is what helps me cope with this solitary confinement so I am addicted to reading more than 10-14 hours a day.

The way the cells are situated I can speak to another prisoner but I cannot see the person I am speaking to. The cells and cell-wing is set up in such a way that you hear and smell everything in your immediate area. It is truly like a zoo. I am in an area now where one of the men is seriously mentally ill. He talks to himself all day and late into the night. Often he screams that he is being raped and acts out the drama over and over again. He talks and shouts about his raping women and children. I do not know if what he is shouting about is something he is imagining or if it is something that has happened. I am often able to block out his ranting and raving but it disturbs others in my area and their reactions I pay attention to because I do interact with them. I had to explain to somehow to disregard his ravings and not allow his torments to drive them insane. Over the years I have been in this situation and worse. There have been times when the man next door would be smearing himself with his own feces and shouting all day and night. I have learned how to shut out the prison sounds and focus on something that I'm doing inside the cell, whether it is reading, writing, meditating, or watching television.

I sleep when I get tired and sleepy. I do not have a set time to go to sleep. I do not sleep deeply because this environment is hell and not home to me. A person must remain on guard and in a semi-sleep state when getting rest/sleep.

When I get to go to the shower I am handcuffed and escorted by guards down the wing and put into a glass shower. We are allowed only three showers a week and the showers are timed. Even in the shower there is no privacy. There is a window that runs the full length of the shower room so that I am always under observation from the guards in the security bubble. The cuffs are removed once I'm in the shower, but the cuffs are put back on and I'm escorted back to my cell.

When I get to go to a visit with my family or friends it is a non-contact visit. There is a plexiglass window between us and we must speak through a telephone to communicate. The visits are under a time restraint and there is never enough time. We are under constant and complete observation by the guard(s) during the visit.

The above is a summary of what my day is like on death row here in Pennsylvania at S.C.I.-Graterford. At times it's worse but never better. I hope this information is useful to you.

Sincerely,
Dr. Qahhar Ali Cush*

*Qahhar Ali Cush currently lives in RHU, a restricted housing unit, at Graterford prison.

24 Hour Death Watch

Jada Wittow

It's the last of everything
last meal, last words
last hug, last smile
last kiss

Appreciate the small things
Live like you are on a 24 hour death watch

You have 6 months left to live, son
the doctors say
a timer ticking in your head
a countdown till the very end
Do you think you can ever really prepare yourself to die?

They had the advantage because they knew their time
Advantage? He said
I say, surprise me
shock me, alarm me
I'd really rather not know

IF THE JURY WAS THE EXECUTIONER

Jada Wittow

There might be fewer executions
if the jury put the criminal to death
if they had to be there to see it happen
they couldn't just vote "yes" to death
and then be done with it

Months later
they'd get another letter
not a jury summons this time
but an execution summons

Please report to the Huntsville Unit
6 pm sharp don't be late
Leave the knives, guns, and mace at home please
just bring yourself
and be prepared
to witness the ending of a life
that your vote decided
didn't deserve to continue
you are the future

PUBLISHED

Lyndsey Grubbs

"Shit."

Suddenly, I noticed how my tongue felt as it finished the "t" and rebounded from the roof of my mouth. I felt the skin on my lips crack at the sudden change in shape, and it was strange to feel my mouth form words. It was even stranger to hear my own voice. I don't need it here, so I keep it on reserve, kind of like those families you read about that have special plates just for Christmas. It's only for certain occasions. Oddly enough, I'd almost forgotten what it sounded like. My own voice was suddenly a memory.

I didn't even mean to let it slip. There just wasn't time to swallow the noise before it came out. Four letters, so quick. They sliced the stale air of my cell, bounced off of my heinously cream-colored cement walls, and came back to settle around me like an unwelcome friend. I guess it's weird how one of the few things that still belongs to me is what bothers me the very most. They can't *take* my voice, but I've taken it myself. When I let it out, it crawls in under my skin – a reminder of who I used to be. It brings with it that tingling feeling – the kind where you know without looking that all the hairs on your arms are standing straight up.

 But the word slipped out before I could stop it the minute I discovered the crack in my pencil. The only reason I found it was the new curve that came when I applied a little pressure. The black piece of lead was definitely coming loose from its wooden surroundings. The tip was beginning to splinter and a tiny crack was forming in the wood.

This little crack mattered. It meant I needed to start applying less pressure, loosening my grip, taking a break. Soon I'd pull back and the tiny black core would fall from the wood and down onto the paper leaving a dirty smudge across my words. Then I'd be left alone, just me and the smudge. Not even the low shuffle of lead on paper there to befriend me.

The pencil shuffle brings me an odd sort of comfort. It reminds me of my time in the tollbooth on Loop 1. There I was, for once in my life, an *official* member of something. It might not have been as impressive as those people with jobs that require degrees from fancy schools, but I finally belonged somewhere. I was part of the Texas Department of Transportation – nametag and all. Back then, I had hours to write. I would sit in the tollbooth and go for hours without a single car passing through. I had nothing but time. No one to talk to, no one to listen to, no interest in reading, nothing to do but write. Loop 1 is, after all, nearly stranded from midnight until sunrise. So, during my shift, the tollbooth was eerily quiet. The sound of pencil scratching paper kept this silence from strangling me. It became an unexpected companion.

And now my pencil, one of the only pleasant things in this god-forsaken place, is breaking. My black and white composition book with my inmate number scrawled menacingly across the top is completely useless without my pencil. When it officially breaks, I'm screwed. My pencil will be gone and unless one magically appears, I won't get another one for a long time. The guards don't take kindly to prisoner requests. Combine that with the fact that my own voice is personally nauseating and the likelihood of receiving a new pencil anytime soon becomes almost nonexistent.

I mean, I'll ask for a new one. The hair-raising sound of my own voice isn't enough to *keep* me from asking. The real problem will come when Officer Shruggs grabs the pencil I have now, tosses it back through the tiny food door of my cell and responds without even looking my way, "Looks fine to me. Figure it out."

So now here I am: Cell 5, Death Row, Allan B. Polunsky Unit, West Livingston, Texas, and officially pencil-less. I'm far from my tollbooth, but with a pretty impressive address nonetheless. At least I have an address now. Before I was arrested, I had starting putting down "Tollbooth #7, Loop 1" whenever I had to give my information. This was mostly due to the fact that I didn't actually have an address. I didn't actually have a home.

I can feel the metal tollbooth seat underneath me. It's still got that gross kind of warm sensation from someone sitting on it before me. Daryl's shift had just ended, so it was definitely him who was keeping the seat so warm. Gross. And, just to make things weirder, I always have to do that awkward booth shift with whoever is working before or after me. There's just no way around it. At some point both people will be in the booth, one trying to enter and one trying to exit, and it will be incredibly uncomfortable. There's no way to avoid it. You're pretty much going to be on top of the other person.

So that's how I knew about Daryl. Daryl and I spent our cozy 30-second switch together. Then I waved bye.

I'm settled now. It's midnight and all is quiet, nothing out of the ordinary. There's a bible in the booth that Joanna must have been reading earlier. I toss it into the drawer with a bunch of other misfit stuff – mostly junk. There's a couple of pens, a crumpled up skittles wrapper, some gross girl book (Joanna again), a stray tarot card and some weird Canadian coins that got thrown out of the toll collection. Above the drawer, there are two buttons. One raises the bar to let cars pass, while the other calls an emergency number. Green and red, both fairly straightforward, both shining at what seems like an unreasonable voltage in this dark Texas stretch of land.

I dig in the back of the drawer to find the journal I leave after every shift. A pair of headlights in the distance suggests that I might actually have a toll to collect. As the car approaches, I watch as the driver starts swerving slightly. This is nothing new – he's digging in his car for money to pay the toll. It happens every time. People are predictable.

He arrives at the window and sticks the couple of dollars out toward me without saying a word. My voice is strong and deep and southern, "Have a good night." With the car's taillights pointing back at me, I go for the journal again. This time, no interruptions. I fold it open until I feel that familiar crease in the spine, flip to yesterday's entry and start writing. I know I could go for hours.

So I guess that's when all this writing nonsense really started: back in the tollbooth. I certainly wasn't any sort of stellar student or writer in high school, just walking across the graduation stage was a huge feat for me. I think my dad would have been proud, but he was already dead. My mom should have been proud, but she was too stoned to know the difference. So, high school came and went without any real accomplishments. Mostly, I was just toeing that dangerous line that would land me in two very different situations: with diploma or without. So it wasn't until after high school, and really through my time in the tollbooth, that I actually started writing.

An added bonus was the privacy. No one knew I had turned into this "soft" writer. Outside of the tollbooth I was regular, smoked-up Wrenn. Inside, I was a writer. It was the ideal situation. In fact, I even started coming to work sober, just so I could write with a sharper eye.

I wrote about everything at that dark end of Loop 1. I wrote about my day, about the idiots that I called my friends, and about how I desperately needed to feel the drugs running through my bloodstream again. I even wrote about *that* day. The beat-up composition book in the back of the drawer of the tollbooth was the first place I told my story. It kept my secret.

When the police found the notebook I couldn't understand why they didn't believe that I didn't mean to kill that little boy. My words were clear. His father, yes. I took the gun in a drug-induced rage and aimed it right at his chest. Even the drugs can't blur the memory of the sound he made the moment the bullet hit him. It was like someone stomped on his chest and threw all the air out of his body at once – he crumpled. The little boy is another situation entirely. His death was the product of a stray bullet – but still another haunting sound. His blood-curdling screams punish me every day.

Sometimes I would sit in the tollbooth and think about what would happen if someone read my stuff, other than the cops obviously. I would look down at my slanted, hard-to-read handwriting and imagine what it would look like for someone else's eyes to scan that exact same page. Would they think it was good? Would they dart across the page without any interest or is there a chance that their eyes could slow to an invested crawl? Am I actually a "writer" or really just an idiot drug addict who was lucky enough to find part time work to support his habit? My best guess is the latter.

Well, none of that really matters now because there's been an unexpected new development in my "Death Row writing." I'm getting published. Before the State of Texas straps me to the gurney, I'm going to get a chance to leave my words behind.

I heard about it just now – through the gruff whispers of two of the row's officers. Officer Shruggs and another younger guard were talking outside of my cell as I was being escorted to the showers. "I hear they'll have to cut out part of his last words in the publication, he was a wild curser," they said.

Publication? This is *too* good to be true.

I wonder if I'll get my own chapter in some part of an important state ledger. That must be how they do it. I'll get a chapter with my name, my crime, and my last words. When I really think about it, I can visualize it - an enormous, heavy book being pulled out of the state library with my name in it. Years from now, someone will blow off the dust, open the book and read about my life, a small portion of which I will have authored. I will be *published*.

For all of this to occur, of course, my next step is to find my voice again. A constant reminder of my past life and mistakes, I've found that it's easier to serve my time in the Texas prison system quietly. There's no need to cause a raucous or try to make friends, or try to build relationships with officers – I'm here to serve my time. For this chance, however, I *will* rediscover my voice. If I have to actually vocalize my last words into a microphone in order to be published, I will find a way to do that. I'll find a way to ease into speaking again – to make sure that my words float away instead of lingering around me as a constant reminder of all of the mistakes I've made.

"Shit."

I said it again. This time, nothing went wrong. I just say it because it's familiar and because I know I won't be shocked by the way my mouth forms the word. The thud of the "t" as my tongue drops, the way that my lips pull together to make an "s" sound, it all makes sense. There's nothing complicated here. As a result, the sound of my voice can shatter into smaller pieces and settle around the perimeter of my tight cell rather than hovering over me. I will surely move on to bigger words, eventually even words that form a sentence, but that is a task that will have to wait for another day.

The next day...

I woke up this morning feeling, for one of the very first times since coming to Death Row, that I had something to wake up for. I didn't immediately wake up *just* to go back on a trip to Tollbooth #7 in my mind. Instead, I knew that I needed to use my time to practice using a voice that had been far too silent for far too long.

My day was further improved when my breakfast tray came sliding through the tiny slit in my cement door. Nameless gloves passed me nearly this exact same meal every morning, but today there was something unusual sitting right beside my square piece of slightly over-toasted brown bread. It was a brand new, yellow, number 2 pencil. Officer Shruggs had finally pulled through for me. Maybe he thought all of my cussing yesterday was some sort of sign that I was "losing" it.

With pencil in hand and a slightly uplifted attitude about my ability to speak without shuddering, I was able to start work on what would become my prison project for the next several months: to create the perfect, "publishable" last words.

From the outside...

The sounds of Wrenn's vigorous writing and speech practicing became an ever-present whisper over Death Row. He would be silent for a time, obviously writing, and then suddenly, muffled sounds could be heard escaping from the inside of his cell. As months went by, Wrenn's obsession with his last words became increasingly obvious. The guards, placing bets over brown-bagged sandwiches, were certain that he would be prepared with the most effective and memorable last words ever heard in the very long history of Texas executions.

Wrenn Kreeger, just moments before, had been strapped by the execution team to a white gurney in the middle of an unnervingly green execution room. A saline drip had already started running into his arm and a black microphone dangled just inches from his well-practiced lips. All of this, a product of a strict sequence of events mandated by the state - this was just like any other execution in Texas. It was a process.

The difference, however, lied in the tangible anticipation plaguing today's execution. The air was thick with expectations: It would surely be a long speech, there would certainly be an apology, the soon-to-be-infamous last words would surely be found later scrawled in Wrenn's notebook.

But when he opened his mouth, out came a strong, southern voice that no one had heard from Wrenn in many years.

"Screw it – just put me in a good spot of the book boys. Call me published."

Wrenn's words were short. Disappointing. Behind his booming voice was a feeling of great defeat. After a years' worth of planning, writing and practicing a valiant last speech in hopes of finally "publishing" a real piece of his own work, Wrenn had fallen into the reality that his final words didn't really matter to anyone. Lying flat on his back and strapped tight to an unforgiving gurney was no way to give any kind of *meaningful* speech. As the leather straps pressed in to Wrenn's skin, they pushed out all of the fight and little bit of self-worth he had left.

But no matter what he said, it would after all still be published. And so it was. Just not in the way that he had dreamed...

The day following Wrenn's execution his final words were posted on the Texas Department of Criminal Justice website. He was added at the top of the list, just another 12-point, red, Times New Roman hyperlink. It gave his name, prison number, date of execution, race, county, and of course a typed up version of his last words. There was no beautiful library. No giant state ledger. No dust to one day blow away.

Today, Wrenn's name lives on in different circles of the Texas criminal justice system. He was the man that *almost* got out a meaningful set of last words. But he, like all the others, ultimately crumpled under the pressure. So really, is it possible? Can *anyone* speak last words that are worthy of publication in something like a beautifully crafted state ledger?

Or is the pressure just too much? Are those yellow, leather straps crushing the hopes of any inmate to ever making a truly "publishable" last statement? If Wrenn could speak now, he would *certainly* think so...

Untitled

Zoé Orfanos

Without any hesitation
she opens the door,
knotted skin on smooth brass.
She ushers in his ragged frame
as he counts excuses
turning over each word
as it catches the light
like a knife.

*   *   *

Without dissention,
twelve mouths shape
a perfectly rounded yes.
They borrow his words,
his leaden gaze:
you deserve to die.

TRIPPING

Adam Bradley

Starr County Prison Cell #2883

This was a place I didn't know and immediately I did not like it. The sky faded in gradient until it turned sheer white at the horizon and blended with the treeline, which also melted into nothing. It gave the impression of thick fog at the edges of the world, a dream-like buzz which was too unreal. It threatened to break the trip and that gave me a jolt in my stomach. The dread that crept in before failed trips was gnawing at my fingers and I flexed them compulsively. I went through the steps--started breathing manually, focused on the smells and the textures, tried to turn the trees true green. They were never quite green. It always frustrated me.

The terror softened to unease and the sky started to solidify. There was always a turning point--a 'click'--where I took control of the trip and I could start to mold and shape and invite in others. This one was like a big fish at the end of the line and it was pulling like hell and I was nervous and I couldn't feel the click coming.

Inhale.

Exhale.

Inhale.

Flex fingers.

"MAY 14TH. IT'S A MONDAY"

This was where the shivering and the panic set in. Little flakes peeled away from the sky and behind was dusty unyielding grey and I knew I would lose it. There was a feeling of incredible loudness but really no sound at all, just the vibration in my eardrums and the front of my chest.

"MAY 14TH."

I laid down in the grass, closed my eyes, and woke up sweating with my hands clenched over my ears. It had been 47 seconds. I was back in the cell.

It was May 12th.

Starr County Prison

"Powers had some kind of fucking conniption fit today."
"Dude's losing it. He gets the axe in..."
"If he makes it that long."
"...4 hours. Honestly. He gave me the goddamn creeps though. Just standing in the middle of his cell for an hour straight with his eyes rolled back. 3, 4 in the morning. Sometimes he'd say shit but it wouldn't make any sense."
"Like when you talk in your sleep."
"Words over words and none of them fit together. Like in those churches where folks start speaking in tongues."
"Crazy."
"They check him for drugs too. As if he coulda snuck anything in."
"Sure as shit *seemed* like he was shooting up."
"..."
"You ever get a good look at his fingers?"
"Hm?"
"There was something wrong with his fingers. Like he tried to scrape his fingerprints off or something. They were all deformed at the end."
"God."
"..."
"Did you ever watch him sleep?"
"Powers?"
"He didn't close his eyes."
"Dammit now you're just *tryin'* to creep me out."
"Aw, is Mr. Night Shift a little nervous? You're the only one in the whole damn building with a gun, my friend."
"Gun don't make no difference when Powers pulls some wacko demon shit and calls Satan himself from his cell. That is a Class A freakshow right there."

"Ha. Guess you'll find out. I myself am making my sweet way home
for the night."
"All over after tonight I guess."
"Yup."
"See you tomorrow, Jeff."
"See you."

May 13 2012. 513 Britton Avenue, Rio Grande City, TX

When Jeff Bloom picked up his things and walked heavily
towards the prison door, jangling his keys in his pocket to give off
the vague air of having *something to do,* about which he was much
more concerned than whatever trivialities might happen in his
absence--going so far in this conceit in fact as to consider high-fiving
the incoming guard as if he were replacing Jeff on a football field--
Jeff made double, triple, quadruple sure that he was leaving nothing
behind. He had a certain way of remembering those things 10 or 15
minutes after he left but he would not be coming back today. Under
any circumstances.

Jeff's face was polished by early May wind as he clambered
into his car, a sunset orange Ford pickup. The left headlight was
out, he noticed. Jaymes Powers had this peculiar way of laughing
where even the most forced chuckle seemed involuntary, bubbling
out of him like

Anyway, Jeff. Anyway. Jeff found himself handling the
gearshift and turning the ignition as if the worn-down truck was his
last and greatest possession on Earth, as if he loved it almost
romantically, and found himself breathing like a man who stayed
underwater just a little bit too long, great gulps of beautiful sweet air.
Everything in his life was a miracle. The road swept underneath him
and he turned the radio up loud enough to make thinking more
trouble than it was worth, and drove home. When Jaymes was a
free man, he was a Bulls fan, and he would always talk about the
time he met Reggie Theus in a hotel, and shook his hand, and
Jaymes got this look like he was seeing something he could never

Good evening, Emma. Oh, not so bad. If ever there was a
man deserved to be put to death it'd be Powers. No, just tired.
Been a long day. Sunday shifts. You know. Did you see the blooms

on Main Street? I love this season, Emma. Sometimes I can't stand being locked up inside all day.

That night Jeff dreamed. He was on guard at the death house, just him and Jaymes. As he watched, two other Jeffs hoisted Jaymes out of his cell and led him haltingly to the chair, strapped his ankles and arms and secured his head with metal and Jeff realized he couldn't move, looked down and saw straps around his ankles and arms. The Warden entered like a ring of smoke, he was also Jeff, and nodded to something out of Jeff's sight. Jeff pulled a lever. Jeff watched through a small window. Jeff felt his head burning. Jeff pronounced himself dead at 12:15 AM.

Bolting up, awake now, shivering. Jeff looked at the clock. 12:17.

September 3 2004. 404 East 3rd Street, Rio Grande City, TX.

My coffee machine wasn't working that morning. I guess that was kind of frustrating. It was sticky hot and hazy and even as I got dressed I could feel dampness on my undershirt. I don't remember what I was wearing. I do remember I didn't eat breakfast because of the coffee thing. It was around 9:15 when I left for work, like always.

The way I felt that morning when I walked out is hard to describe. There was nothing in my mind. I mean nothing. Not even a buzz or a song from the radio or anything. Pregnant silence. Like the eye of a hurricane. The street was totally deserted--I was one of the few people in the neighborhood with a job at the time--and it hummed in the heat.

The night before I had taken 850 milligrams of crystal meth through my left arm. I watched "The Rugrats" on my 12-inch living room TV. The whole time I was filing my nails and after a while I looked down and 3 of my fingers were bloody. I had filed about 3 millimeters off my right index finger but I couldn't feel anything. It was just another meth trip. I remember I thought at the time that there might be someone watching me through my TV so eventually I covered the screen with a blanket and left the room. It was just another meth trip. Anyway by the morning I was fine. Probably still

a little hyped up but I'd been to work on a full-blown trip before
and this was nothing.

The gas station is connected to the owner's house via a
complicated series of doors in the back and that's where I went first
to drop my bag and put my lunch in the fridge. He wasn't there.
There was a note on the last door--the one actually opening into his
kitchen--that said "Jaymes--Will be back by 11. Stay out of trouble.
Running low on 5's. Jose".

He left me these letters a lot. I think this meant he was
getting breakfast at Denny's. He almost never worked on Fridays.
He would be gone for hours and I would usually shoot up around 3
and the high would peak on my way home. I dropped my things
and walked out to the register and flipped the sign in the window to
"Open" and started reading Sports Illustrated. Still there was
nothing in my head.

Down Main Street a bit from the Exxon is a narrow brick
building--falling apart like everything else in town--that houses karate
classes for kids. Like self-defense kind of stuff. So lots of times we'd
get parents walking into the Exxon with their kid in his white-on-
white karate uniform and whatever color belt he had and buying
soda or candy or some other reward for going to karate classes.
You'd have to buy 8-year-old me a lot of Twix to convince me to go
to karate classes. I'm just saying. When they came in I'd always say
something like "Better watch what I say around this guy!" and do
the Bruce Lee ninja pose with my arms making an X and my fingers
extended and the parents would laugh politely and the kid would
half-smile because he did not give two shits about karate and was
really just in it for the candy. I admired those kids for doing what
they had to do. Sometimes you have to get your hands a little dirty
to get what you want.

This particular day there must have been some kind of
"graduation" or whatever you would call the last day of these kids'
candy racket because there were well-dressed parents and
uniformed little kids streaming into the Exxon around noon. I was
still definitely a little high at this point and I was rapping my fingers
on the counter and arranging and re-arranging displays and talking
under my breath. I must have seemed a little crazy at the time. But I

can't have been crazy yet because there was still nothing in my head. That was just the meth. The craziness was different.

The karate crowd filtered back out to cars and bikes and I took a shuddering breath and walked to the back. I remember thinking I needed to sit down and just feel the tops of my legs. If I could just do that then I would calm down. That was my first conscious thought since I had woken up that morning. I went through the doors back to the kitchen to sit down.

I still do not understand how this kid found his way into the kitchen. Like I said you have to go through 3 different doors before you get there, and they're all marked "Staff Only" and there aren't any lights. Either this kid had done this before or he was a brave fucking explorer. It doesn't make sense to me now and it didn't then either. When I walked into the kitchen he seemed like he was just looking. Just wanted to see what was behind that door. Still wearing his karate uniform. He was a yellow belt. I didn't know what that meant but I figured they were all just bullshit since the kids aren't old enough to actually hurt anybody in the first place. I figured he was about 9. Turns out his ninth birthday was in a couple weeks so I was pretty close. Later I learned his parents had walked out of the Exxon in a conversation with another family and didn't notice he was missing until a few minutes later.

I don't think he immediately realized I was there but he jumped and turned around pretty quick. He was maybe 4 and a half feet tall and had this scruffy black hair that hung over his forehead. His face reminded me of pictures of Native Americans I had seen: he had a long angular nose and a bony chin and a very kind of solemn look. At this time I was about 6'2", 275. Real overweight. Probably kind of intimidating even to a kid who knew some karate. We looked at each other for about ten years before he swallowed loudly and said "lo siento". "Lo siento". Sorry. He said it over and over and I just looked at him not really knowing what to do. My head was back to the incredible vast nothing it was earlier. I had this feeling like I had made up my mind about something, but I couldn't figure out what it was. A decision had already been made.

He said "lo siento" again and he was crying a little bit as I just stood there blocking the door and suddenly it was like every single thought I hadn't been having came flooding into my head and it almost physically hurt. I think I staggered a little bit. They were like a cloud of insects and I couldn't distinguish between one thought and the next but the first one that floated up coherently was of a story I'd seen on the Internet a few months earlier. I won't say where. I don't want this pinned on them. Don't want people saying "Well Jaymes Powers read such and such website and look what it did to him". It was coincidental. I don't even remember if this was true or claimed to be true or if it was some sick fiction or what. The guy said he had killed this girl, about 10 years old, to see what it felt like. She would come into his apartment to watch TV and one day he just hit her in the head and suffocated her on the floor. I remember that when I read it I wasn't disgusted or horrified but just kind of banally interested, like you'd be interested in a painting at a museum. I hadn't given it another thought until that moment. And then I realized what the decision was that had been made.

The kid had I guess given up on me moving from the doorway and now he was crying softly and asking for his parents in Spanish. I crossed the room with a couple steps and reached over his head--I noticed he was shaking--and grabbed a cutting board off the drying rack. This is where I think I mix some things up. He started apologizing louder and getting a little panicky. I stepped back and I said "what the fuck" and hit him as hard as I could in the head with the cutting board. The noise he made was completely unreal. I've never heard anything like it before or since. It was a kind of shriek that sounded more scared than you can imagine. He fell over holding his head--he wasn't bleeding yet but that first hit definitely cut him. At this point he was still apologizing--"Lo siento! Lo siento!"--but I don't think he really even comprehended that he was saying anything. It was like when I would hunt deer, and right before they died there was this look in their eyes like they were seeing something they could never understand and it had completely overcome them and then they were gone. "Wild-eyed". That's the look this kid had. Miguel. His name was Miguel.

I couldn't believe the first hit didn't knock him out. He was on the floor shaking and crying and yelling how sorry he was. That's the part that really stuck with me--he was so sorry. I wanted to scream at him "I'm the one who should be sorry! What the fuck did you do?" but instead I took the cutting board and smashed it

into his head again. His head rebounded off the tile floor and now
he was unconscious. All the thoughts that had washed into my head
30 seconds ago were gone again. It was the most profound silence
in my head. A perfectly still ocean. Now there was blood pooling on
the floor and the kid's wrist was twitching but he was definitely still
breathing and alive. He was on his stomach and I turned him over.
His face was a mess. I think his nose was broken. His breath
sounded bizarre and unnatural, like there was no rhythm or
anything to it. I looked around the kitchen. Everything I did was
smooth and efficient and powerful and there was no thought behind
it at all. Like some kind of animal impulse was telling me to do what
I did next, which was take a bag of apples out of the fridge--it was
the heaviest thing I could find--and whip it down on his face like a
chain-ganger breaking rocks. He was dead after that. It took a few
minutes. I watched his breathing stop through his karate uniform.
His face was just nothing but blood. That looked bad.

I didn't really know what to do now that it was done. I
didn't feel bad about it or worried that someone would catch me. I
was definitely worried about the mess I'd made in my boss's
kitchen. There was blood and hair all over the floor and no one was
going to be able to eat those apples. I would have to change my
shirt. Apparently I stood there looking out the kitchen window for
30 minutes before Jose walked in with a carryout bag. I don't
remember.

**Transcript of an Interview with Judge Victor Gonzàlez, 5th Circuit
Court**

INTERVIEWER: What was your impression of Jaymes Powers
during the trial?

GONZALEZ: Unstable. Obviously. Jittery from withdrawal. But
when he spoke he was comfortable and warm and soft-spoken. Not
in a menacing way either. Genuinely shy and ashamed a little bit, I
think. Not so much ashamed of the murder itself as he was
ashamed of inconveniencing so many people with the trial. He
reminded me of a child who's gotten caught doing something silly
and trivial that he knows he shouldn't do. And when he gets
punished he's upset and sorry but also frustrated that the whole

thing had to happen at all. That's the feeling I got from Mr. Powers.
He wished it would all [unintelligible]...it would all just go away.

INTERVIEWER: Did you feel that Mr. Powers deserved the death
penalty?

GONZALEZ: Absolutely.

INTERVIEWER: How long did the jury deliberate?

GONZALEZ: Twenty minutes. They barely had to leave the
courtroom. That's very unusual. In a capital case. There tends to be
one or two anti-death penalty jurors in even the most disgusting
cases. Prosecutor did his job on jury selection.

INTERVIEWER: Elaborate a little on your view of the death
penalty.

GONZALEZ: It's been around for centuries and I think it's right.
It's an expression of the will of the people. When you take a life,
you should expect to surrender your own. That's justice. Also
frankly it's logistically necessary in this part of Texas. Prisons are
overcrowded and I think you only exacerbate problems when you
throw convicted murderers into packed jail cells. The Powers case
was a great example of why we need capital punishment. A drug
addict committing motive-less killings should be put to death. This
isn't a sentiment I ever vocalize in court—

INTERVIEWER: Of course.

GONZALEZ: [unintelligible]...for obvious reasons.

May 20, 2012. Starr County Death House.

I do it because I like seeing them die. You can write that
down. I'm a diagnosed sociopath. Used to be a schizophrenic but
we got better. Ha! That one kills me. I can only work at certain
hours of the day because of the position of the sun. I'm an Aries.
There are certain times of the day--it's a long explanation. I'll go on.
I was the executioner for Jaymes Powers. Killed by lethal injection

six days ago in this death house. Really satisfying job. One of the best in a while.

He was basically catatonic when they walked him into the chamber. Had these eyes staring for miles and miles like he was back on meth. I heard he did meth when he killed that kid. I didn't have any trouble finding his veins either. His whole arm was red and pockmarked. Really added an extra layer of awfulness to him, the drug addiction, so that was good. We strapped him in--13 seconds, fastest team in the state--and I took a hair off his head, like I always do. Do you want to see?...later. He didn't even blink. So in went the IV and this guy's still just burning holes in the ceiling like he was concentrating real hard on something none of us could see.

So of course the next step is we ask them, "Do you have any last words?" and a microphone comes down from the ceiling and usually it's a sadsack apology or a Bible verse or something. Lotsa Bible guys get executed. Never understood that. Well, I asked Jaymes Powers "Do you have any last words?" and damned if he doesn't say, straight to the ceiling, "I'd rather be dead". He took a breath like there was more but that's all he said. "I'd rather be dead". All I could think was "you've come to the right place!" Right? We all laughed about it afterward.

Now this is my favorite part and I don't want to mis-tell it. I'd just gotten the go-ahead to start the first drip which knocks them unconscious so they don't die looking at a bunch of goons leaning over the table to make sure they're dead. So I leaned over to start the chemicals flowing, and Powers makes this motion like he's trying to lift his arms (couldn't, obviously) and says real sweetly "I have to leave now. But I will love you forever." Still staring at the ceiling, let's recall. "I have to leave now"! Like he was running to the goddamned grocery store for Fig Newtons and Coke! All of us on the team just kinda looked at each other funny and shrugged it off. Apparently this guy was a loony-toon on death row too.

Then he was out. His eyes stayed open even when he lost consciousness. Don't see that eeriness too often. I started the drip on the paralytic. Finally I sent in the big dogs--ha!--and waited for his last breath. I wish a lot of times at work that I could film these. Something very satisfying and reassuring about watching lungs stop

moving. This guy, Powers, right in the very second his last breath
shuddered out of his chest, a tear fell diagonal down his cheek. Like
it got forced out right at the end. I went for high-fives but the team's
been avoiding those lately. Apparently a month or so ago we had a
federal inspector in to observe and they found it unprofessional.
Some shit. We all just did a great thing. Have some goddamned
respect and let us celebrate.

Time of death 12:15 AM. Good night.

May 14, 2012. Starr County Death House.

I spent all day Monday deciding where to go. So many
places and events were overplayed and I couldn't go out bored. I
decided I would get married. I needed the trip to be perfect. Friday
was still rattling around in my head. That couldn't happen again.

Where to have the marriage was the easy bit--I always knew
I'd get married in Spain. There was a line in a Beatles song about
getting married "in Gibraltar near Spain". I thought about inviting
the Beatles. At least John. I'd think about it later. There would be a
big archway that we'd walk under in the grass and no dress code.
The women would be in their prettiest sundresses and I would be
barefoot. I might even invite Miguel. I've wanted to have this girl--
Alicia Breiton--since I was 12 and it looks like this is my last chance.
If I time the trip right we might make it to the honeymoon. I don't
know. I don't want to rush things. But it has to start now. 8:30 PM. I
start pacing.

It usually takes 20 laps of the cell before the hum starts.
There's a buzz in either ear that makes thinking too hard and I stop
completely. This is why it has to be immaculately planned before I
get in too deep. It's hard to rally my mind for changes once I'm in,
even after the click.

It's all coming so easily this time. Soon the details of the
wedding become electrical pulses, surging from the front to the
back of my mind. The visuals come in differently with every trip.
This time it's really clever. Snapshots of my wife and I, like in a
scrapbook, and on the last one it melts into a real scene and here I
am, and there's the arch and the girls in sundresses and Miguel is

there in the second row. His face is beautiful. And Alicia is coming down the aisle created by the folding chairs and she's beaming and I can't believe how perfect this trip is. I'm supremely concentrated and focused and I feel smooth and efficient and powerful. It reminds me of another day.

Let's start the vows. The chaplain is my father. I haven't seen him outside of a trip since I was 8. He looks about my age now. "I do"s. We kiss. The sun is so bright here. Alicia gives a playful nibble at my earlobe as we hug and sway and whispers, "Don't ever leave me". I kiss her neck and say "I'd rather be dead." The people are all gone. The Beatles never came. That was a misfire in preparation. It's just Alicia and I. And Miguel. Miguel in his chair still.

Fuck fuck fuck. The sky is melting. Fuck. This trip can't break oh God. Stay with me a few minutes longer. The wedding is gone and now it's just Alicia and Miguel and I and we're suspended in whiteness and this great expanse of nothing. This is my mind. This was my mind when I killed Miguel. I can't tell if the trip is stabilizing or not. Alicia seems content to just look at me. She's murmuring "I love you" in a singsong kind of lilt. Miguel is saying sorry.

The most miraculous feeling is coming out of my heart right now. Literally flowing through my arteries. Like my insides are outside of me. I'm not making much sense. It's like every part of me is breathing. I'm more alive than I've ever been. I look down at my body and it's Miguel's body. Alicia is still here and I grab her wrist and stare her in the eyes and yell "I have to leave now". I have to yell because there's this deafening static all of a sudden. The feeling of loudness.

I remember from Friday.

I just need another minute.

"But I will love you forever".

What I'm seeing right now I could never expla

12:15 AM, May 14 2012. Starr County Death House

"Somebody should close his eyes."

"What if he needs to see something, wherever he is?"

FOOD FOR THOUGHT: THE PRISON CHEF

Elizabeth Rademacher

People ask me all the time,
Lou, what would your last meal be?
That's what they usually ask, at least,
When they learn where I work.

But after 20 years in this kitchen
Cooking dish after dish for the about-to-be dead
These questions taste bad in my mouth.
They take away my dried up appetite.

Some inmates ask for a king's feast:
Whole pizzas, juicy steaks,
Gallons of ice cream, golden fries.
One asked for a full Thanksgiving dinner once.

Others are minimalists. A glass of water,
An orange, a bowl of cereal.
They aren't too fussy.
Some just don't care anymore.

It can be hard when you're cooking
For thousands of people every day.
But this is a menu for a party of one
So I try to chop, fry, and grill with care.

But I can only work with what's in this bleak pantry,
Like canned beans that used to be green
And some poor, gaunt chicken breasts.
And each time my mind starts to wander.

They say that the richness of taste and smell
Creates the most powerful memories of all.
What does this meal conjure up in Walter Black's mind?
How does anybody possibly decide?

With all the kindness I have I set down the tray,

Wishing I had better ingredients to work with.
And at 3:45, when the meal is being carried away,
I am still left wondering.

How does anybody possibly decide?

FRIED CHICKEN

Elizabeth Rademacher

Bouncing from one foster family to the next
Did something to shrink my appetite. They told me,
*"You are an extra mouth to feed.
You are a burden to us. You are worthless."*

But Mrs. Watson was different.
She was thin and wrinkled like a leaf
But she was a strong oak tree of a woman.
And Lord, could that woman cook.

My first night in her tiny house
She set the table, took me into her kitchen,
Where she turned ugly pink scraps of chicken
Into crispy, juicy pieces of heaven.

With flour, eggs, and breadcrumbs
She made those wings crackle and sizzle
Until they were consecrated
From food into warm, edible love.

The taste of the meaty muscle and
Savory, perfect skin danced across my mouth.
For just a second, maybe less,
The house smelled like mom was there.

But Mrs. Watson's heart was too full.
Two months later, it just stopped beating.
And from the bright light of her house
I was sent back into the darkness

To punches and shouts,
To needles and empty bottles,
To days dodging school and cops,
Until I looked in the mirror

And I saw my father looking back at me.

THE LAST MEAL

Elizabeth Rademacher

It's 4 o'clock sharp.
Like cruel clockwork,
The guard brings a tray
And sets it down next to me.

Frozen, I stare. Is this a dream?
Because it can't be real.
Gingerly, I pull the tray closer
While the guard watches and waits.

It isn't the feast I imagined it would be
But even if it were, it wouldn't matter.
My mouth is dry like a desert.
This is really my last meal. The end.

I hold the plastic fork, numb and still.
There are limp beans more gray than green,
A puddle of flaky mashed potatoes,
And a slice of a chocolate cake, no candle.

There is no comfort for me in this food,
But what really makes my stomach churn
Are the scrawny chicken wings, the grizzled,
Sizzled limbs lying helplessly on the plate.

Grizzled, sizzled limbs that remind me
Of my own dark arms and legs,
Parts of a body that in two hours' time
Will be strapped down and fried in a chair.

I see myself on this plate.
A disappointment, a waste,
Made from cheap, bad ingredients,
Something that no one would want.

I thought they would give me strength.

But now I can't bear to touch them.
We're the same. We'll be thrown away.
There isn't much longer to wait.

READERS DIGEST: THE JOURNALIST

Elizabeth Rademacher

I've written too many headlines
And I've seen too many men killed.
And each and every time, readers care most
About what their last meals were.

Their times of death, their crimes,
Even their last words on this earth are
Almost irrelevant, overshadowed
By a few sentences about what they ate.

Some people think it's because we all ask,
What would I eat if I could pick my last meal?
But I don't believe that's the whole reason.
It's something deeper than that.

When people read the newspaper tomorrow,
They will say Walter Black was self-made monster,
Ignoring or perhaps forgetting his shattered past
Of old scars and wounds that never healed.

They'll read that he ordered his favorite meal,
And they'll think he still had control over his life.
When they read that line, they'll assume Walter
Deserved every volt of his electric death.

And that's what the state wants you to think.
But if people walked a lifetime in Walter's shoes,
Or if they knew that even his last meal
Wasn't totally within his own control

Then what would they think?

We don't put that information in the news, though.
Because most people don't want to think
Of these kind of men as other human beings
Who have been chewed up and spit out.

It's a fact most would rather not digest.
Because then they would see a bit of themselves
In a cold-blooded killer. They'd see someone
Waiting to be thrown away.

THE PRACTICE OF KILLING

Story by Robert Johnson

Adapted for the Stage by Marc Estes and Robert Johnson
2012

Setting: Death row. A cell equipped with a bunk and a steel toilet. The cell sits alone with a large space between it and an electric chair. Above the elective chair hangs a single light bulb.

At rise: BILL Donovan, dressed in prison clothes, sits alone on his bunk. His face is buried in his hands. The stage is in complete darkness except for the light bulb over the electric chair. A spotlight begins to weave around the stage like a prison search light. After a brief time, the spot light finds BILL and expands on him as the lights come up over his cell.

BILL

(Lifts his face from his hands with a sigh, he turns to address the audience.)

How would you feel if you were sitting in the death house, waiting to go? I never dreamed I'd end up here. I want out but really, there's no way out for me. Not now. Maybe not ever.   I put myself here. Now I've gotta see it to the end.

(Pause, takes a deep breath)

My heart's been pounding in my chest for hours. Am I gonna hold up? I gotta walk to the chair, not crawl. Or be carried. I worry about that. I mean, wouldn't anyone wanna show a little dignity, even in the death house? There's nothing left now between me and the chair.

(Rises and looks in the mirror above the toilet)

36

(Faces audience as keys and chains rattle off stage)

You'd think I'd be over it by now, but every time I hear the keys, I shake. Maybe tremble's a better word. Gets me right up on edge.

GREEN
(From off stage) (sound of footsteps approaching)

Donovan!

BILL
(Walks to cell door and holds the bars)

Funny how these bars are meant to give society some sense of security as long as the bad guy's behind them. Now they give me security from what waits on the other side. Waits and watches.

(Rests his face between the bars)

They give me some, I don't know, some relief. Bar's to a cell are cool, cool to the touch. Cold comfort. I hold 'em close. Helps me stand up straight, maybe stand up to what's coming next.

(Pulls his face back)

No sense in struggling. I'm way outnumbered. Heard one guy got his goddam arm broke putting up a fight. Didn't do no good. It's over now. Soon. Real soon.

(Sinks his head)

(GREEN approaches with the WARDEN and another OFFICER)

GREEN

This is what's goin' down Donovan...

BILL
> *(Head bowed, he interrupts)*

I know what's going to go down.

GREEN

All the struggling in the world ain't gonna change the outcome. It's gonna happen.

BILL
> *(Resigned)*

No struggles

GREEN

> *(Looks at him in a moment of compassion. He sighs.)*

Hands

> (BILL puts his hands through the tray slot in his cell door allowing GREEN to cuff him up. The lights begin to fade as BILL is pulled from his cell and the other officer shackles his ankles. GREEN straps his arms down with a leather belt. The spotlight goes on BILL as he again addresses the audience.)

BILL

I remember when they killed McVeigh. I sat on my couch like most other people that had their TV shows interrupted for the special coverage. I remember thinking how he deserved it. Looks different now, harder to figure, not so clear cut.

> *(Lights come back up)*

WARDEN

Son, I've got a job to do.

> *(WARDEN begins reading a death warrant. His
> voice softens as the lights fade and the spot light is
> on BILL again.)*

"This is to command the warden of the State Penitentiary—that's
me, son—to carry out the execution of said subject by means of
electrocution on the day and time indicated herein..."

BILL

> *(To audience)*

Said subject? Sad subject? Soon-to-be dead subject? Is this how it
goes? The words are cold, hard. Who knew? I know now, and I
can't stop thinking about what it'll feel like, strapped tight to the
chair, leather mask covering my eyes and mouth, me fightin' to
breathe right. It's a tight fit in that chair. Will I panic? Maybe
everybody does, just you can't see 'cause the guy's strapped down
tight, real tight. Man, how'd I let things go this far?

> *(The lights come up. The WARDEN folds his
> paperwork and puts it in his inner coat pocket.
> Another officer enters.)*

WARDEN

It's time to go.

> *(The two officers each take a side and GREEN
> takes the back, holding onto a belt loop in BILL's
> jumpsuit. The WARDEN leads the way.)*

BILL
> *(Stops)*

You know...

> *(Shakes his head in resignation)*

Never mind.

> *(Continues walking. The walk is somber as the
> lights dim; a bulb over the chair gives an eerie
> illumination to the group. The officers guide BILL
> to sit down. Five more officers enter and make a
> semi-circle behind BILL.)*

> *(Sitting, he addresses the audience)*

Eighty-five years of death right in this seat. Justice. Nothing
personal. Just trading humanity for a number. And maybe an
unmarked grave.

OFFICER

> *(Moving into position to strap BILL's leg.)*

I do the right leg.

BILL

The right leg? What am I, a goddamn piece of beef at a butcher
shop? "I do the right leg." What'ya say to that?

> *(The officers remain silent as they continue to strap
> him tightly to the chair. One officer tightens the
> final strap around his chest, puling quick and tight.)*

Jesus!

> *(He sighs, trying to regain some breath.)*

> *(Looking around the room)*

Peeling paint and the odor of mildew, sweat, and fear. This place
even smells like death. .

> *(To audience)*

You... you get to sit in the witness room. How comfortable are you? I'm all alone. It's me and the chair; me in the chair. Even in this room full of people, you people, looking at me real close, I'm all alone. Do I have any last words? What should I say? What could I say? Does it really matter anyway? I suppose not. I'm not the person I was before all of this.

> *(A mask is lowered over Donovan's face as the stage lights dim to blackout. After a brief pause. GREEN speaks out of the darkness.)*

GREEN

Cut! That's a wrap!

> *(Lights come up on the scene to the laughter of the OFFICERS and the WARDEN)*

Welcome to the Rock View Prison's Execution Team, Bill.

> *(OFFICERS quickly un-strap BILL from the chair.)*

WARDEN

You're in Donovan.

> *(Handshakes begin all around.)*

BILL

No sweat.

> *(Bills voice cracks a bit.)*

GREEN

Still think you can handle any assignment in the prison? Taking a man to his death, even if it's a direct order of the court, man, it's

unlike anything you could ever experience. You got that now,
right?

OFFICER

Things like this build empathy.

BILL

Empathy, my ass... Well, maybe. It's not something I'll forget,
walking to the chair like that.

> *(All freeze but BILL, who makes his way to the
> front. BILL addresses the audience.)*

I suppose I'll be a better officer in the death house, now that I know
what a condemned man goes through. Hell, I'll certainly watch'em
like a hawk... Maybe that's the real point of all this. Green's right.
This is the toughest job an officer could get. This is the real deal.

> *(Pauses as he looks to the ground and then looks
> back up at the audience.)*

Justice... Justice can be a bitch... but that's life. If you can't take the
heat, stay out of the death house.

THE END

REFLECTIONS FROM A MURDERER

Alexandra Olson

October 6, 2009

Today was fun. I brought the brothers to the electric fence that's outside of the school. You know how in the cartoons, the little guy gets electrocuted? He shakes, his hair spikes up, and steam comes out of his ears. I've always wondered if this is *actually* what happens if you get electrocuted. Why not try it on my brothers? LOL. So, I took out the video camera and dragged my brothers out to the fence. The stupid boys didn't want to do it. They got too scared. But they didn't have a choice, hehe. I told them that it would be like "Jackass"; it would be funny. Anyway, I got my brother on tape. It was hilarious. He's like...a peanut. And he touched the fence for just a couple seconds and then BAM fell to the ground, shaking. So hilarious. I ended up touching too. It hurt like a mother! But I didn't fall to the ground like my pathetic brother. Anyway, I'm going to make a youtube video out of it. Make sure you look for it! ;)

Last night, Jennifer and I went to this party. Jennifer was way weird last night. I pulled her aside cuz I had this crazy thought. I was like, "hey, Jenn, I wonder what it would feel like to kill someone" and she was so taken aback! Like seriously? I was just saying! It doesn't mean that I'm actually going to do anything. I just thought it would be something interesting to talk about. Whatever. Jenn just said that that was a weird thing to say. THEN, she got weird again. Jenn told me that she's going to have this killer Halloween party this year. I told her that I could totally hook her up with some drugs. Again, she freaked the fuck out. She was like "since when do you do drugs?" and shit. I mean, I thought it was kinda obvious ever since Rob and I have been dating. She was all "no, don't bring drugs to my house". I dunno. Jenn is being weird. She better get over herself though. She's not being the friend that I need her to be right now. Not cool.

– Alyssa

October 11, 2009

    I was the center of attention in the bus today, as always (lol). My one friend was filming our bus ride home. I was screaming and swearing at the top of my lungs. Just fucking around. It was whatever. But I got this weird feeling on the bus. My little sister was in the front of the bus with this neighbor of ours. I think they're best friends or something. And I couldn't help but wonder how it would feel to beat that girl. Or slit her throat. You know what I mean? I mean, what does it feel like to actually slit someone's throat with a knife? What kind of sound does it make? How bloody is it? I couldn't stop thinking about it. I think the girl's name is Elizabeth or something.

    Then, as usual, I got home and had to do a shit ton of chores. My damn grandparents never let me do anything. They're way too strict. Honestly, I can't wait until they die. Is that bad to say? LOL. They are just so strict! They never let Rob come over. Grandma says that he always smells weird and that she gets a bad vibe from him. They are gonna die sooner or later...I'm just waiting for it to happen so I can do whatever the hell I want.

- Alyssa

October 14, 2009

    My goddamn phone died because I lost the pathetic charger for the thing. I'm super depressed and fucking angry, too. It'd be nice if I could call Jenn or Rob. I'm someone that needs to talk, you know? If I don't talk about it, I bottle it up, and when I explode someone's going to die.

- Alyssa

October 17, 2009

Yo. I have been having a blast coming up with a plan to kill my fucking neighbor. Dude, being completely stoned makes you think wicked things. So here's what I decided: I gotta start digging. I'm gonna make little Elizabeth a grave. A nice grave in the forest. I'll make it about a mile away. AND here's the best part: I'll make TWO graves. Just to make it seem like I have a thing for digging. Like it wouldn't be weird at all that I'm digging. You know what I mean? Then, I'll have Emma asked Elizabeth to come over and play. I dunno why she would say no – they're best buds. Then, I'll tell Elizabeth that I have a surprise for her in the forest (that way no one would be able to see what was going on). I'll lead her to my spot, where I would have already set up the shovel (to beat her with) and knife (to slit her throat with). I've got this covered. This is crazy, but it's gonna be fucking awesome.

Things kinda suck otherwise though. I wanted to hang out with Rob...or maybe call Jennifer. I dunno. I kinda need someone to talk to right now. I'm not feeling right. I mean, it's almost the anniversary of my suicide attempt. That always trips me up. I always go back and forth between wishing that those damn pills had killed me and being glad that they didn't. It's weird. Oh well, I can't call anyone now anyways (still no charger). So, what do I do? Okay, don't judge, but I totally pretended to get pissed off at Emmy just so I could punch her in the stomach. That made me feel better, LOL.

–Alyssa

October 21, 2009

I just fucking killed someone. I strangled them and slit their throat and stabbed them and now they're dead. I don't know how to feel at the moment. It was ahmazing. As soon as you get over the "ohmygawd I can't do this" feeling, it's pretty enjoyable. I'm kinda nervous and shaky though right now. Kay, I gotta go to church now...lol.

– Alyssa

October 23, 2009

I still haven't gotten rid of that feeling – the shaky one. I feel like my stomach is twisting and turning nonstop. I'm so fucking nervous. I really did enjoy what I did, but I'm just super nervous now. The police are looking for Elizabeth. They're looking all over the place. They started at my house because that's where Elizabeth was seen last.

Detective dude: About what time did Elizabeth come over to play?

Me: It had to have been around six or so. It was just after dinner.

Detective dude: And what time did she leave your house?

Me: She only stayed for a little bit. She said that she had to do some homework or something.

Detective dude: So, about what time?

Me: Oh, uh, probably seven-ish.

Detective dude: Right. And which way was she headed?

Me: You know, I thought she was going home, but now that I think of it, she headed down towards town instead of next door. I'm sorry I didn't think of it before, I guess I really didn't think anything of it.

Detective dude: Thank you. Miss Alyssa.

And that was that. On his way out, the detective dude saw one of the holes that I dug up. He stopped and looked at it for a while, then just walked away. That scared the shit out of me.

– Alyssa

October 24, 2009

I don't know what made me do it. I was just sitting in class and everyone has been talking about Elizabeth and how weird everything is. I dunno. I fucking turned in my diary entry. You know, the one that says that I fucking murdered Elizabeth. And that I *liked* it. Dude, I'm going to die. Like, I'm actually going to die. I have no idea what this means, but shit. Shit. Shit. Shit.

– Alyssa

October 31, 2009

Going into juvie. I'll be there until I'm 18 (three whole years). Then I get tried in court. That's when they decide what to do with me. I'll be in jail, at least. I'll be in chains as I walk down to face the judge. I'm leaving tomorrow fur juvie. I don't have anything to do. All I can say is that I think I fucked up.

– Alyssa

January 28, 2012

I gave up writing for a while there. Now, three years later, I'm back to where I was. Except I go into court in two days. I'm 18 – I'm now death eligible. How insane is that? Death eligible. They'll decide whether or not I should be sentenced to death. Or given life, with or without parole. I'm not sure if there is hope for life from this point on. Come to think of it, I let go of any trace of hope when I decided to kill Elizabeth. My attorney is spending hours and hours over documents that have my name written all over them. He's trying to find a way to say that I'm insane. You know, "parents neglected her as a child", "raised by very strict and unsupportive grandparents", "clinically depressed", "suicide ideation", "attempted suicide more than once", blah, blah, blah. The judges will talk among themselves "oh yes, she is pretty fucked up, isn't she?" and they'll debate whether or not I acted out of insanity or not. But for some reason, I have this gut feeling that it's already too far gone.

The hope is gone. My life ended with Elizabeth's. What stupidity.
Happy fucking birthday, Alyssa.

- Alyssa

January 30, 2012

I've never seen so many reporters, cameras, microphones,
flashes, and chaos than today. Everyone wanted to know what I
looked like. Everyone wanted to know what "the monster" looked
like. I walked into the courtroom in hideous lime green jail clothes,
my hands pulled and locked in front of me. I made my way down
the aisle of the court room. It was kinda weird because it reminded
me a lot of church. Except I wasn't walking down the aisle for
communion or to celebrate a wedding or whatever. I was walking
down to hear what my sentence would be: death or life? Then I saw
her. I saw Elizabeth's mom. My attorney told me that she would be
there. My attorney told me to "keep my cool" and remain
"respectful and mature" when I saw her. But goddamnit, I couldn't
keep my cool. When I saw how broke she was, there was no way I
could keep my cool. Absolutely not.
        The judge called on me. Guilty or innocent? Earlier, I pled
not guilty. But then I realized later how fucking stupid that was. I
mean, they had my journal entry. Ya, I'm clinically depressed, but
does that justify what I did? I decided that no, it doesn't. so, I got up
and said "guilty". I told Elizabeth's mom that I was really, truly
sorry. I told her that if I could take Elizabeth's place so that
Elizabeth could live, I would do it. In a heartbeat. I later found out
that my words meant nothing to Mrs. Olten. I read in the paper that
she said that "so much has been lost at the hands of this evil
monster" (evil monster being me, Alyssa). She actually said that I'm
"not even human" and that she hates everything about me. Being
called a monster may not seem like a big deal. But when it's real, it
has a whole new meaning. Mrs. Olten is right. I was...I am a fucking
monster.

- Alyssa

February 8, 2012

I got my sentence. I guess the minimum I could've gotten was 10 years. I got life with parole. In thirty-five years, I'll go back and try to defend my case. But for now, I'm here. In jail. Elizabeth's mom said something that stuck with me. She said that Elizabeth "was given the death sentence and we were given a life sentence". Worded that way, it seems odd that I was given life when Elizabeth, the innocent one, was given death. I had a damn good attorney who argued about my mental health affecting my behaviors. At this point, I don't even know what should have happened. I'm so far detached from this whole thing now that I'm in prison. Prison life is rough and it's only just begun.

I have a really small cell. I guess they're all pretty small. I have a toilet, a sink, and a cot. I have my diary and my pens. The other inmates kind of scare me. They've all been through some pretty rough shit. But I'm definitely one of the youngest people here. They all heard about what I did. In a way, I think they're kinda scared of me. For these people – these prisoners – to be scared of me? Well, that means something. And that's not good.

– *Alyssa*

March 29, 2012

Elizabeth haunts me. It's strange because I know that I haunt her family way more than I can imagine. I'm that "monster" that killed their once perfect life. I say that I'm sorry; I say that I would take her place in a second; but none of that means shit. None of that means anything because none of that can happen. What's done is done.

I remember everything in such great detail. I remember her expression right before I put my hands around her tiny neck. She didn't understand why I was doing that. Her face showed pure innocence and confusion. She couldn't understand why in the world I would put my hands around her neck. I remember feeling her heart beating – at first so incredibly fast that I thought it was going to burst. I was ready to see blood pouring from her chest due to her heart's explosion. And her squeal. She squealed and gasped. And her heart started to slow...down. I felt it get less and less powerful as my grip around her neck tightened. When the beating stopped, I was in a trance. I picked up the knife. I remember the sound. It's nothing that I can explain. It was a squishy and gushy sound. The blood. Oh my god, the blood. I have never witnessed so much blood in my entire life. It was all over my hands, mixing with the dirt, staining her shirt as well as mine. I was shaking as I rolled her into the girl's grave and covered her with the bloody dirt.

I made a mistake when I was fifteen years old. And I'm punished for it for the rest of my life. All I can say is that I deserve it. Every single second of this goddamn life in prison. I deserve it.

– Alyssa

April 20, 2012

This is my last journal entry of this old life. My therapists and friends have been saying that I have to make this life my own again. It's kind of hard to do when you don't really think that you deserve to live. It's a tough balance because I know that I fucked up. What I did is beyond permissible in any way, shape, or form. At the same time, I'm terrified to be put to death. What a strange paradox. I deserve to die but I don't want to die. Elizabeth didn't deserve to die, nor did she want to die. This world is messed up, and I'm greatly to blame for its continued hostility. I fucked up and I don't understand how to maintain the courage to continue living. But I have to maintain at least some kind of hope for a life that may happen in the future. I realize that I'm nowhere near understanding the full extent of what I did. But that's what these next thirty-five years are for

See you on the flip side.

– Alyssa

"Purple" in Three Parts

Zoé Orfanos

Part One: Lavender

Frank West ran his fingers through his graying hair as he re-read the newspaper clipping. When he'd finished, he read it again. Leaning against the window frame, he released a sigh. Without looking he knew the lawn's exact shade of green and how many feet back the little shed sat on the property. Inside the shed, he imagined the lawnmower resting against left wall, the toolbox Luke had given him for father's day, and the rusted pink bicycle leaning against the back wall. He inhaled until his chest felt tight.

His wife Lisa had left the clipping on the seat of his worn, leather recliner before leaving for her nine o'clock appointment. Frank's fingers combed through his hair as he looked back at the small, grey square of paper.

Jennifer West, 26, passed away among friends and family at St. Agnes Hospital on Tuesday the fifth. A talented artist with an overwhelming heart, Jennifer's largest passion was her family. A devoted daughter and sister, Jennifer is survived by her mother Lisa, her father Frank, and her brother Luke. The family will be holding an open gathering today at Finnegan's where Jennifer worked as a hostess for the four years. Please come between 2 PM and 6 PM. Please wear purple.

Frank blinked. Suddenly he saw her: long blond braids and three shades of purple, leaning against her bike. New and slick, the bike's little green ribbons swayed softly from the handle bars. He had taken her photo, a giggling frosting-faced grin by her birthday balloons.

The sound of the front door lock brought him back to window. Setting down the little gray paper, he turned toward the door.

"Frank?" a tired, female voice drifted toward him. She found him before he could respond. Lisa's dark brown hair was curled back tightly in a damp bun. Her lavender cardigan hung open over her jeans.

"Did you eat? I'm sorry I didn't leave you anything before I left." Frank flinched.

"I'm sorry, that's not what I meant." Lisa turned away, walking into the kitchen. "I'll make you something now."

Frank glanced back at the clipping. He quickly tucked it into his back pocket before following his wife into the kitchen.

As the bacon omelet slid onto the glass plate, the phone rang. Frank answered the phone in the front hallway. When he returned to the kitchen, Lisa had set the table with two plates, each covered by omelets and toast.

"It was Marcy." Frank sat automatically, speaking into his omelet. "She's bringing by the photo collages for the reception. She wants our approval." Frank sank his fork into the eggs.

"She's been such a blessing. I really can't thank Marcy enough. Did you know she organized the entire reception at Finnegan's? That girl acts more like her sister than her closest friend."

Frank nodded absently as he meditated on the clipping in his back pocket.

Part Two: Plum

Marcy parked her little blue Ford on the edge of the driveway. She glanced at her phone on the passenger's seat. The little red light had been blinking for six days. It would be Jennifer's voice. She hadn't listened to the voicemail since she received the unnerving call from Jennifer's mother. *She's at St. Agnes. He hit her again. Come now.* Sitting by Jennifer's bed, the little light had been the only movement in vaguely-colored hospital room. Jennifer reached for her phone and shoved it in her purse.

Opening the door behind the driver's side, she pulled out three large, laminated poster boards. Dozens of faces smiled from each poster. Though each board was covered in photos, little hints of purple paper peeked through. Marcy secured them under her arm and turned toward the house. She smiled at the familiar red brick. From the driveway, she could see the two bare spots in the lawn, made from two sets of feet swooping down from plastic swings. Though the swing set was long gone, Jennifer had never let her father re-seed the patchy grass.

Marcy continued up the driveway. Approaching the door, she shifted the posters against her plum-colored top and stiff, black skirt, reaching to ring bell. The door swung slowly open.

"Marcy, dear! You're an absolute doll to be doing all of this." A tall, thin woman embraced Marcy in a tight hug. The woman's grey roots highlighted the rigid part in her hair, drawn back in a glossy bun.

"Anything for you, Mrs. West." Marcy noted the bags under the woman's eyes and the unbuttoned cardigan. Mrs. West hadn't put on her makeup yet today.

"Well, come in, sweetie! Put down those posters so we can see them."

Marcy was acutely aware of Mr. West leaning against the far wall of the front room. Crossing toward a sofa, Marcy propped the posters against the pillows.

"Here they are. I printed out those baby photos you sent me and mixed them in. I think we got her at every age."

The pair stepped back as Mr. West drifted over to stand behind them.

His voice was soft. "Marcy, they're perfect."

The two women jumped.

"Thank you, Mr. West. And thank you for that photo of Jennifer with her bike. It was perfect. I blew it up to be the largest photo." Marcy pointed toward the middle poster.

He returned a tight smile before turning to look out the window.

"Is he coming to the reception?" Marcy's question froze both Mr. and Mrs. West in place.

Mrs. West's voice came out in a whisper. "If that horrible human being even *tries* to—"

"We're not sure." Mr. West finished. "We didn't extend him an invitation, but as you know, the reception's a public event."

Marcy nodded. "Are you driving to the restaurant, or would you like me to pick you up at 1:30?"

Mr. West turned from the window, "We'll drive, Marcy. But thank you for all of your help. The posters are wonderful."

The three turned back to stare at the giggling little girl on the bike. Mrs. West pulled the edges of her cardigan closed, blinking away a tear.

Part Three: Black

All of the mahogany tables had been pushed up against the wall. The matching chairs with their emerald green cushions were stacked neatly in the corner. A note was taped over the open sign to read "Open to those who loved Jennifer." The guestbook lay prone on the hostess' station.

Mark shifted awkwardly in the doorway. No one had seen him yet. He'd parked four blocks away and walked past the rows of cars that lined Shaw Street. Finnegan's was packed. The low lighting illuminated the murmuring purple crowd. Mark looked down at his light grey polo and black slacks. He drew in a quick breath and crossed into the room.

He was pulled up short by Jennifer's smile, multiplied dozens of times across several posters. Jennifer smiling with Marcy at their graduation; Jennifer and her family at Christmas two years ago; Jennifer at her college graduation; Jennifer cutting a magenta cake at her last birthday party. Mark had been standing next to her when she'd cut the cake. He was nowhere in the collage.

His throat tightened. Jennifer was gone. Closing his eyes, he saw her blond hair spilling out over the sofa cushions as she laid on her back, reading a book, her legs dangling over the arm. *How can you read like that?* He'd asked her that question since he met her in high school. She had only ever laughed in reply. Closing his eyes more tightly, the picture shifted. Jennifer's hair was tied loosely back and her smiling face grew pale and angry.

"How could you say that to me? How could you say I'm not working hard when I work overtime *every week* just to support you?" Her face began to flush as her voice rose, "You're twenty-six, Mark. *Grow up.*"

His arm had moved toward her without his permission.

"What are you doing? Get your—get your hands *off*—"

Now both of his hands were on her.

"*Mark.*" She was screaming, her arms striking uselessly.

And then he saw her eyes. His hands jerked open as he stepped back. Suddenly unsupported, she staggered backward falling headfirst into the corner of the coffee table.

He stood still, staring at his twitching hands. Nothing else had moved.

He felt a hand pinching his arm.

"What are you doing here?" Marcy hissed in his ear.

Mark turned toward Marcy and stared. He couldn't move.

"Get *out.*" She began to push him. "*Now.*"

He began to move toward the door. Marcy shoved harder. As the posters retreated from view, he tried to memorize her smile. By the

time her smile disappeared completely, he couldn't see anything.
His hands were shaking too much for him to wipe away the tears.

56

INNOCENCE

Philip Cardarella

Innocent until proven guilty.
The state's threat to take it away.

But Innocence isn't an argument, but a truth.
Not an opinion, but a fact.
Not a title earned, but a title lived.

Innocence
Not completely understood.
Not easily proven.
Not always shown.

Because our system is made
Of human eyes
Human ears
Human minds
And one truth unites all things human
Being human means being wrong.
Sometimes, always, but never never.

A system always human.
A system not always humane.
A system can always rule guilt

But can never take way
The truth of innocence
The fact of innocence.
The title truly lived.

Innocence can never be taken.
But the innocent life can.

THE COST

Philip Cardarella

What is execution worth to you?
A sense of safety?
A satisfaction of sterilizing a stain from society?
A slightly sounder sleep?

What is the cost of execution?
And I don't mean money.
I mean the real cost.
An innocent life?
Two?
A hundred?
Maybe more?

No.
The real loss is our humanity.
Our self-respect.

Because how can we respect ourselves
When killing Cameron Todd Willingham
Means a little more sleep
Instead of a little less.

**These poems were based on the case of Cameron Todd Willingham, a man who was put to death by lethal injection in 2004 after being convicted of murdering his three children in a house fire. Five years after his execution, investigation experts found that the evidence that convicted Willingham was inconclusive and could have been used to acquit him, if he was still alive.*

Nobody Shot Jim Crow Dead

Monica Sok

just a few Trayvon Martins
walking in the neighborhood,

just a few Troy Davises
sitting on death row

just a few more hooded boys
strolling in the streets

just a few more unreported
black-on-black crimes

just a few more wars on drugs
near your mama's house

just a few more black men
in handcuffs at the station

just a few more generations
to talk at the dinner table

about Buddhist teachings,
when Uncle Josh says,

"Life always
has its suffering

so you have to learn
to let go."

And no, that's not happiness
that's contentment, you know.

Maybe letting go means
you've got to bend back
the bars from the window,
so that our children can swing on them.

TROY

Monica Sok

First his veins,
then his muscles,
last his heart.

Justice for few,
Justice for some,
Justice for none

Before and After

Monica Sok

The bars glide and bend
gently from a pointed top,
clasping at the bottom
of the cold dirt floor.

A hinge on the side
flaps open a small door
that only unlocks when
the key is jagged with the word: Now.

Too many people inside that bird cage
yesterday, today, and tomorrow.
Everyone slamming against the bars,
shoulders dislocated,
slinging.

We fought before, we'll fight after.
We struggle to push the bars
until, finally, a man
can live a new life.

About the Editors and Contributors

CLAIRE CALLAHAN (Editor-in-Chief) graduated *summa cum laude* from the honors program at American University in December 2012 with a degree in Law and Society and a certification in French Translation. Through independent research and a teaching assistantship in Professor Robert Johnson's honors colloquium, The Death Penalty, Callahan devoted her undergraduate studies to the investigation of the death penalty and solitary confinement both at home and abroad. In September 2012, she presented an original short story about bullfighting and capital trials entitled, "Why the Corrida," to the European Society of Criminology in Bilbao, Spain. Callahan plans to attend law school after gaining work experience in social justice non-profits and professional French translation.

ROBERT JOHNSON (Consulting Editor) is a Professor of Justice, Law and Society at American University, Editor and Publisher of BleakHouse Publishing, and a widely published and award winning author of books and articles on crime and punishment, including works of social science, law, and fiction. He has testified or testified expert affidavits on capital and other criminal cases in many venues, including US state and federal courts, the U.S. Congress, and the European Commission of Human Rights. He is best known for his book, *Death Work: A Study of the Modern Execution Process*, which won the Outstanding Book Award of the Academy of Criminal Justice Sciences. Johnson is a Distinguished Alumnus of the Nelson A. Rockefeller College of Public Affairs and Policy, University at Albany, State University of New York.

ADAM BRADLEY (Author) Adam Bradley is an undergraduate honors student at American University's School of Public Affairs. He is currently pursuing an interdisciplinary major in communications, law, economics, and government. He has worked as a Congressional intern and as an editorial intern at *Poet Lore*, the nation's oldest poetry journal. His choice of reading material vacillates between David Foster Wallace and health policy, but he has always loved writing stories, especially stories that have never been told before. He hopes to pursue a post-graduate degree to teach high school English.

LIZ CALKA (Cover Design) is a DC-based, award-winning designer and photographer with a degree in Visual Media and Graphic Design from American University. As Art Director at BleakHouse Publishing, she has designed covers and layouts for a number of BleakHouse publications including books and magazines. She also created and maintains the BleakHouse website.

PHILIP CARDARELLA (Author) Philip Cardarella is an alumnus of American University, where he graduated summa cum laude and received a Bachelor's Degree in Political Science, a minor in Communication, and a certificate in Advanced Leadership Studies. He is a member of the national honors society Phi Beta Kappa and won the School of Public Affairs' 2012 award for Outstanding Scholarship at the Undergraduate Level. He will be returning to American to pursue a Master's Degree in Political Communication.

QAHHAR ALI CUSH (Author) Dr. Qahhar Ali Cush, born in Philadelphia, PA, under the name Robert Lee Cook, Jr. graduated from the American International University of California with a Doctorate degree in Philosophy in 1995. He completed his Master's degree in Christian Theology at the Bethel University of the Watchtower and Track Society in New York. In 1996 he obtained his paralegal certification in Corporate Law from the Professional Career Development Institute. His work as a Jailhouse Lawyer has been instrumental in helping many gain their freedom or reduction in their sentences. He has a passion for reading and writing. Poetry and short stories are his specialties, whether the creations are his own or whether he is simply enjoying the works of others. Since 2003 he has begun painting as a way to express himself. His artworks have been shown in art showcases from the East Coast to the West Coast. His large family and many friends are of the utmost importance in his life. Cush is a Commissioned Officer in the N.O.I. and U.N.O.I.

MARC ESTES (Author) is a two-time winner of the Vermont Playwright's Award for his plays, "What Would Dickens Do?" and "Glass Closets." "What Would Dickens Do?" went on to win the 2012 Robert J. Pickering Award for Playwriting Excellence. His play, "Gumbo," was a finalist in the 2011 Safe Streets Arts

Foundation short play competition. Estes is a native of New Hampshire and graduate of the University of New Hampshire.

LYNDSEY GRUBBS (Author) Lyndsey graduated from American University in December 2012 with a BA in Public Communication and a minor in International Studies. Lyndsey's Senior Capstone project, laying the foundation for "The Troy Davis Foundation," also focused on the death penalty in the United States. She is currently working as a Publicity Assistant in Corporate Communications for Discovery Communications.

CARLA MAVADDAT (Cover Design) is the Assistant Art Director and Curator for BleakHouse Publishing, an award winning photographer, and an undergraduate majoring in Political Science at McGill University. She is originally from Montreal, Canada, but grew up in Washington, DC. Mavaddat has a passion for photography and design, along with a longstanding interest in human rights and social justice. Her creative work has appeared in several venues, include *Adore Noir*. Mavaddat has served as Editor for the 2011 and 2012 issues of the online literary magazine, *BleakHouse Review*, which features a distinctive noir aesthetic.

ALEXANDRA OLSON (Author) is a merit scholar and senior Psychology and Spanish Language student at American University. She is heavily involved in psychological research and received the Killam Fellowship to continue her research in Montreal. Upon graduation, Alexandra plans to attend a Clinical Psychology program to obtain her doctorate.

ZOÉ ORFANOS (Author) Currently abroad at Oxford University in England, Orfanos is an undergraduate student at American University in the School of Public Affairs. She graduated High School with both an International Baccalaureate and Honors diploma and is currently working toward a Bachelor's degree in Law and Society with minors in Creative Writing and Literature. Orfanos achieved the BleakHouse Best Poem award for her poem, "Lethal Rejection, A Poetic Adaptation" which appeared in the last edition of BleakHouse Review. Last year, Orfanos served as the Editor-in-Chief of the 2012 Tacenda Literary Magazine.

ELIZABETH RADEMACHER (Author) Elizabeth Rademacher is a senior at American University in Washington, DC, majoring in Law and Society with a minor in Psychology. Rademacher has previously worked with the American Bar Association's Death Penalty Representation Project and is passionate about civil rights law. An occasional poet and avid reader, she plans to attend law school in Fall 2013. Her last meal poems included in this issue were selected from a poetry compilation she wrote entitled, "You Are What You Eat."

MONICA SOK (Author) graduated from American University in 2012 with a B.A. in International Studies. As a Cambodian American, most of her writing draws from issues of identity, cross-cultural understanding, and her family history during the Khmer Rouge regime. Sok is passionate about poetry and empowering others through creative writing. In the near future, she hopes to pursue a MFA in poetry.

SONIA TABRIZ (Text Design) is a merit scholar and J.D. candidate at The George Washington University Law School, where she is Editor-In-Chief of the *Public Contract Law Journal*. Tabriz graduated with honors and *summa cum laude* from American University with majors in both Law & Society and Psychology. She received the Outstanding Scholarship at the Undergraduate Level award from American University for her award-winning works of fiction, legal commentaries, artwork, presentations, university-wide accolades, and academic achievement. Tabriz is the Managing Editor of BleakHouse Publishing.

JADA WITTOW (Author) is an undergraduate honors student at American University majoring in Justice and Law with a concentration in Criminology. Her interests include Juvenile Justice and Social Work. Her poetry appeared in BleakHouse Review (2012). The executioner poetry Wittow wrote that is included in this issue was inspired from a meeting with Jerry Givens, a former executioner in the state of Virgina. Wittow is currently studying abroad in Rome.